P9-CSH-993

Toot & Puddle
The One and Only

by Holly Hobbie

LITTLE, BROWN AND COMPANY
New York ~ Boston ~ London

Little, Brown and Company

Time Warner Book Group
1271 Avenue of the Americas, New York, NY 10020
Visit our Web site at www.lb-kids.com

First Edition: September 2006

Library of Congress Cataloging-in-Publication Data

Hobbie, Holly.
Toot & Puddle : the one and only / by Holly Hobbie.— 1st ed.
p. cm.
Summary: Opal shares her frustrations with Toot and Puddle when the new girl at school, Bubbles, starts imitating the way she dresses and steals her ideas for class projects.
ISBN 0-316-36664-1
[1. Pigs—Fiction. 2. Imitation—Fiction. 3. Schools—Fiction.] I. Title. II. Title: Toot and Puddle. III. Title: One and only.
PZ7.H6517Toch 2006
[E]—dc22 2005012852

10 9 8 7 6 5 4 3 2 1

SC

Printed in China

The illustrations for this book were done in watercolor.
The text was set in Optima, and the display type was set in Windsor.

PIG
TALE

There was a brand-new pupil in Opal's class when school started in September. "My name is Jane," she said, "but I want everyone to call me Bubbles."

Jj Kk Ll Mm Nn Oo Pp Qq Ss
WELCOME BUBBLES

For some reason, the new pupil latched onto Opal. She shadowed Opal around the playground during recess. She squeezed in next to Opal at lunchtime.

Bubbles seemed to like Opal so much that by the end of the week she was even beginning to dress like her.

"Gee whiz," Daphne said, "she's wearing almost exactly what you're wearing."

"I guess Bubbles likes my outfit," Opal said.

Opal told Toot and Puddle all about the new pupil the next time she visited Woodcock Pocket.

"She's drawn to you," Puddle said reassuringly, "because you're so pretty and smart and friendly."

The week before Halloween, everyone worked on their costumes during art period. Opal decided to be a monster. "I love to be scary," she said.

But Opal was not the only monster at the Halloween party. "I love to be scary, too," Bubbles said, growling in her disguise.

"What a wonderful costume you've created, Bubbles," said their teacher, Mrs. Haze. "You're doing so well in our class."

Daphne was annoyed. "Bubbles copied your costume, Opal. How can you stand it?"

That weekend at Woodcock Pocket, Puddle explained, "It's just because Bubbles is new at school and not sure about what to do. Once she feels more at home, she will do things her own way."

"She must think you're good at everything," Toot said.

"But what about Mrs. Haze?" Opal asked. "Didn't she see that Bubbles copied?"

"I'm sure Mrs. Haze just wants to encourage her new student," Puddle said. "Teachers have to do that."

COOK
BOOK

For Thanksgiving Opal wanted to make Mrs. Haze a special card. She drew a tall, handsome Pilgrim riding a very colorful turkey.

When she gave her teacher the card, Mrs. Haze said, "Oh, thank you, Opal. What a coincidence, Bubbles gave me a card, too. And you both had the same idea."

"Really?" Opal said. "That's incredible."

"What's incredible, dear?"

"Oh nothing, Mrs. Haze." Opal didn't want to be a tattletale.

As the days grew wintry, the air tingled with excitement. Everyone in class made paper snowflakes for their holiday projects. Most of the snowflakes were quite different, but Bubbles's snowflake was a lot like Opal's.

Mrs. Haze gave them both gold stars.

Daphne said she'd never known someone who was a copycat *and* the teacher's pet at the same time. "That stinks."

"Bubbles can't help it if Mrs. Haze likes her," Opal said. She thought that was probably what Puddle would say.

When Opal told the snowflake story on her next visit to Woodcock Pocket, however, Toot was flabbergasted.

"The one who copied got a gold star, too? Holy moly!"

"Never mind," said Puddle calmly. "We all know who made the most beautiful snowflake."

All winter Bubbles had been wearing a distinctive red wool hat. Everyone knew it was a prized gift from her aunt.

Daphne spotted the exact hat in a holiday catalog.

"Let's give Bubbles a taste of her own medicine," she said to Opal.

She ordered two.

"Opal, I love our new hats!" cried Daphne.

But guess what happened next?

"Oh my! It looks like you've started your own fashion fad, Bubbles," said Mrs. Haze.

"I know," Bubbles said. "Isn't it exciting?"

Then came Valentine's Day. Opal drew Cupid as a little piglet and called him Cupig. Bubbles thought that was a wonderful idea. "But the picture should be bigger," she declared boldly.

Everyone was most impressed by Bubbles's giant Cupig. "You are so clever," Mrs. Haze said, smiling.

And Bubbles received the biggest pile of Valentine's Day cards in the class.

Daphne couldn't believe it. "I've never known anyone who was a copycat *and* the teacher's pet *and* the most popular in class. That's impossible."

"I think it's possible," Opal said, rolling her eyes. "Everything seems to go her way."

Well . . . maybe not everything.

For the big theatrical extravaganza in May, the girl students in Mrs. Haze's class decided to be in a chorus line. Everyone did quite well at practice—except Bubbles. She was always out of step. No matter how hard she tried, she couldn't get the rhythm right.

Opal took her aside. "Watch me, Bubbles, and do exactly what I do. It's not that hard. Hop, step, and kick! Hop, step, and kick!"

Bubbles did exactly as Opal did—"Hop, step, and kick!" she cried—and sure enough, she was soon dancing.

"That's it," Opal cheered. "You're getting it."

"I'm getting it," Bubbles squealed.

"Bubbles is getting it," Mrs. Haze announced to everyone. "Thank you, Opal, thank you. How marvelous!"

“Why do you want to help Miss Copycat?” Daphne asked.
“Because I want our chorus line to be perfect,” Opal replied.

Indeed, the chorus line was the sparkling climax of the night's entertainment.

And the brightest star of the evening was the one and only Opal.

"Bravo," cried Puddle.

"Hooray," hooted Toot.